WHERE DID THEY GO?

a spotting book

Emily Bornoff

In the hot desert among sand and thorns,

something is moving with long, twisted horns.

Where is he hiding? Maybe you know?

Where did the sandy-haired addax go?

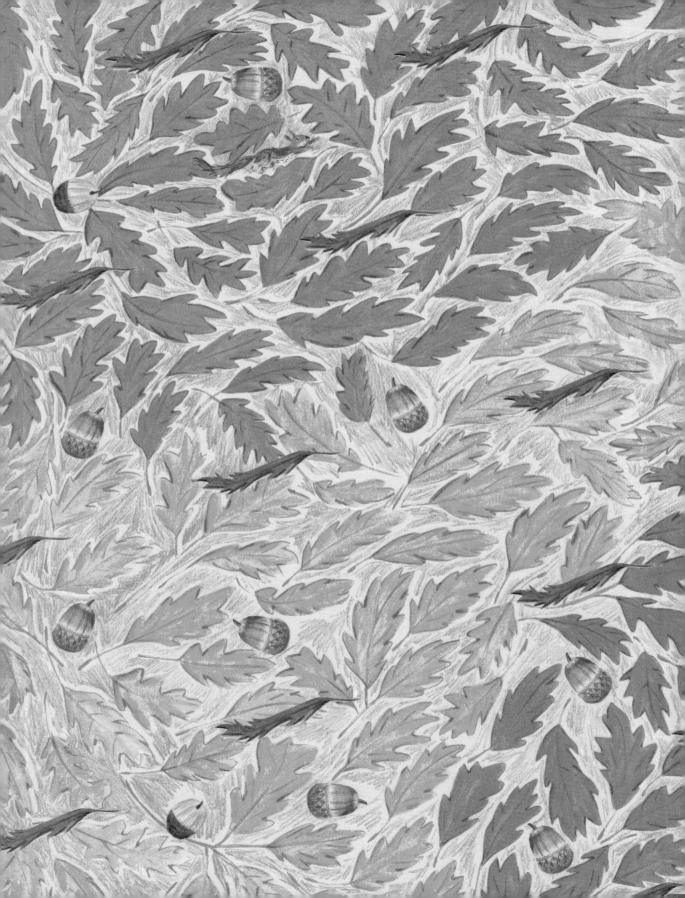

Deep in the forest as autumn takes hold,

a creature is dancing in leaves, red and gold.

She's looking for acorns to store and to stow.

Where did the bushy-tailed red squirrel go?

The dusty Great Plains are this animal's home.

Where is he hiding? Where does he roam?

Is he lost in the tall, waving grasses that grow?

Where did the broad-shouldered bison go?

Up in the clouds near the blue of the sky,

a mother and baby are somewhere nearby.

Are they high in the mist or somewhere down low?

Where did the mountain gorilla go?

In branches and leaves is there anything here?

With three-fingered toes and long, dark-brown hair.

He's not moving fast for he's known to be slow –

where in the world did the sleepy sloth go?

A creature is under the shady gum tree,

she has long pointed ears and a tail – can you see?

She digs in the earth to escape the sun's glow.

Where did the burrowing bilby go?

This slow, gentle giant carries his home
around on his back in the shape of a dome.
Over the islands he plods to and fro.
Where did the giant tortoise go?

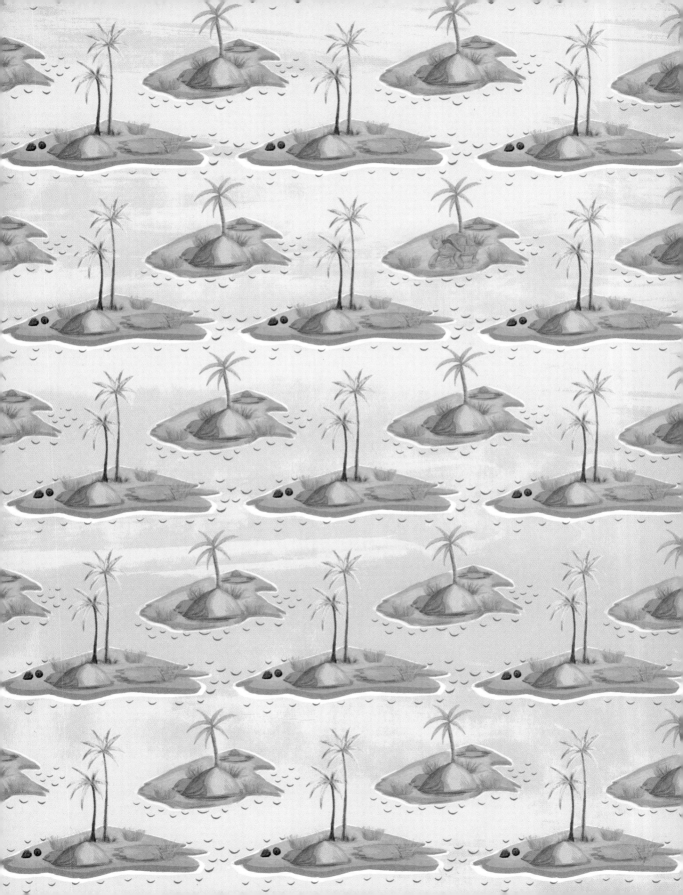

This horse with stripy black-and-white hair,

could be hiding anywhere.

But if you look closely, maybe she'll show.

Where did the galloping zebra go?

You'll shiver with cold in this frozen place,

where ice sheets cover every space.

But something lives here in this land of snow.

Where did the fish-loving polar bear go?

If you listen at night you may hear a howl,

as through the green cacti this hunter prowls.

She's searcing for food as the cold winds blow.

Where did the ghostly grey wolf go?

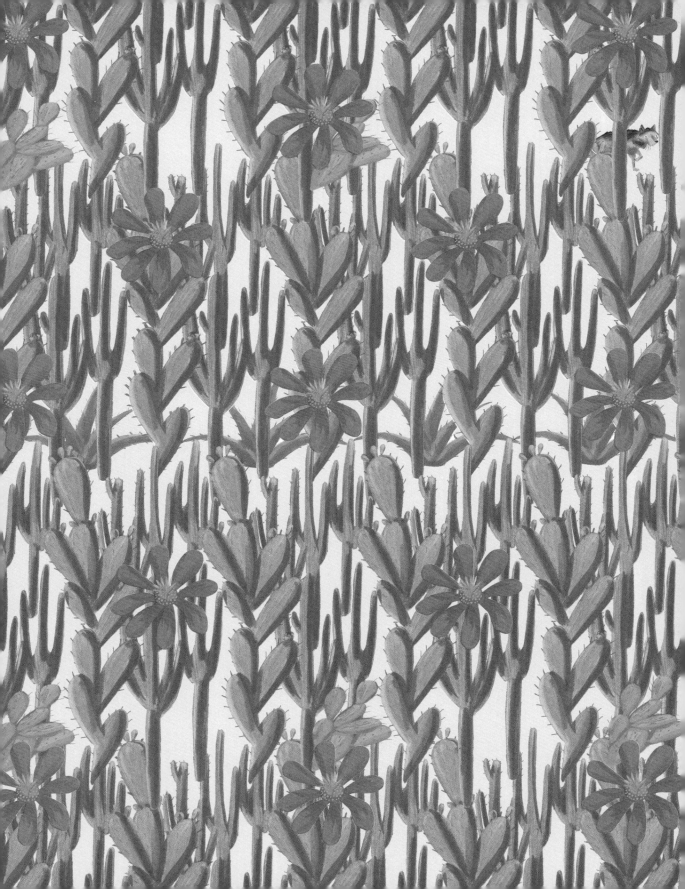

What can you see where the wide river floods?

Is he deep in the water or wallowing mud?

He'll be somewhere here in the great river's flow.

Where did the snappy-nosed gharial go?

This big hungry bear loves

tall green bamboo.

She eats it all day —

how much can she chew?

She's somewhere close by with

black eyes and black toes.

Where did the round-bellied

giant panda go?

A snuffle, a snort, can be heard round about.

There's an animal here with a very long snout.

We can hear him nearby –

leaves are rustling and so,

a tapir is near – just where did he go?

All round the world in
deserts and seas,
in mountains and rivers,
just where can they be?
They are hiding in forests,
on plains and ice floes.
Where are they now?
Where did they go?

Where did they go?

Did you find all the animals?
In the wild many of them are very hard to find.

ADDAX
Addax used to be found right across the Sahara Desert, but they are hunted for their horns and there are fewer than 300 left.

MOUNTAIN GORILLA
Mountain gorillas are found high up in the thick forests of central and western Africa. These forests are being destroyed and there are only around 700 mountain gorillas left.

RED SQUIRREL
Red squirrels are still common on mainland Europe, but the larger, stronger grey squirrels have almost completely replaced them in Britain.

SLOTH
Sloths sleep up to 20 hours a day, and sometimes algae grows on their fur! The South American rainforests where they live are being chopped down.

BISON
Bison can weigh over a ton. Millions of them once roamed the grasslands of North America, but huge numbers were killed by 19th-century hunters.

BILBY
Bilbies are unique to Australia. Newborns stay in their mother's pouch until they are 11 weeks old. They are threatened by introduced predators like foxes and cats.

GIANT TORTOISE

Giant tortoises live on the Galápagos Islands, and weigh up to 250 kg. They nearly became extinct when people brought egg-eating animals into their habitat.

GREY WOLF

Grey wolves can hear a wolf howl 6.4 km away. Mexican Grey wolves are the smallest of all grey wolves and were hunted to near extinction in the US.

ZEBRA

Grevy's Zebras live across the savannas of eastern Africa. Each zebra has a unique pattern. More and more cattle are being grazed on the grasslands, leaving less food for zebra herds.

GHARIAL

Gharials live in the rivers of the Indian subcontinent. They have over 100 razor-sharp teeth, and a long, thin snout. Fewer than 200 gharials may be left in the wild.

GIANT PANDA

There are fewer than 2,000 giant pandas left. A panda can eat up to 38 kg of bamboo every day, but their bamboo forests are being cut down.

POLAR BEAR

Polar bears have adapted to live in the icy arctic. Under their white fur they have black skin to soak in sunlight. They are threatened by warming oceans melting the ice on which they live.

TAPIR

Malaysian tapirs have lived in the Southeast Asian forests for millions of years, but are under threat from habitat loss. Tapirs have a nose a little like an elephant's trunk.

To Mum, thank you for your never ending support
and to those who ensure all the endangered animals
in the world are protected – EB

BIG PICTURE PRESS

www.bigpicturepress.net

First published in the UK in 2015 by Big Picture Press,
part of the Bonnier Publishing Group,
Deepdene Lodge, Deepdene Avenue, Dorking, Surrey, RH5 4AT, UK

www.templarco.co.uk

ISBN 978-1-78370-278-7

Printed in China

This book was typeset in Brown.
The illustrations were created digitally.
Written by Katie Haworth. Text on pages 30–31 by Josie Skillman.
Designed by Amanda Newman/Perfect Bound Ltd.